Items should be returned on or before the date shown below. Items
not already requested by other borrowers may be renewed in person,
in writing or by telephone. To renew, please quote the number on the
barcode label. To renew online a PIN is required. This can be requested
at your local library.
Renew online @ **www.dublincitypubliclibraries.ie**
Fines charged for overdue items will include postage incurred in recovery.
Damage to or loss of items will be charged to the borrower.

Comhairle Cathrach
Bhaile Átha Cliath
Dublin City Council

**Leaeharlanna Poiblí
Chathair Bhaile Átha
Cliath**
Leabharlann Shráid Chaoimhín
Kevin Street Library
Tel: 01 222 8488

| Due Date | Due Date | Due Date |
|---|---|---|

D1344772

**PROMISES**

I ♥ Glitter Boy
by Julia Clark
Illustrated by Georgina Fearns
Published by Ransom Publishing Ltd.
Unit 7, Brocklands Farm, West Meon, Hampshire GU32 1JN, UK
**www.ransom.co.uk**

ISBN      978 178591 254 2
First published in 2016

Young
Adult

# Julia Clark

Ransom

♥

# Wednesday
## 4th May

I wish we all lived on a mirror ball. The world would be a far happier place.

Yup, that's my theory: the world needs more **BLING**. And less **BORING**.

'Lily Turner, you're bonkers! Tone it down.'

That's what Ally always says. Of course, she's talking about my clothes.

Ally is my BFF. She should know by now: I **love** bling.

So, today I wore …

❋ A top with silver sequins.
❋ Jeans with shiny bits down the side.
❋ A sparkly belt.
❋ Shoes with a starry design.
❋ A matching star in my hair.

Crazy, I know. But that's me.
That's my world.
Everything is shiny and perfect.

♥

# Thursday
## 5th May

**OMG!**

My shiny and perfect world turned upside down today.

I'm not sure what happened.

OK, perhaps I do know.

Today I met a boy.

He's not shiny like that dude from the Twilight books. Edward Cullen or whatever.

But he is perfect.

**OMG!**

♥

# Friday
## 6th May

Correction.

I didn't actually *meet* the boy yesterday.

I saw him from a distance.

He transferred to our school.

He's got ...

* A movie star's smile.

* A movie star's skin

      – not a zit in sight.

* A movie star's build.

*AND*

* Muscles like you won't believe!

I saw him again today.

OK, perhaps I stalked him a bit.

I found out his name is Mark Ward.
A name fit for a star!

Ally saw him too. She rolled her eyes
at me.

'Close your mouth, Lily,' she said. 'And stop staring. *Jeez!*'

But I couldn't stop.

He is **such** a hunk. Better than the other boys at our school.

I'll won't see him again until Monday.

How will I ever get through the weekend?

♥

# Saturday
## 7th May

Missing

    my

        movie

           star.

♥

# Sunday
## 8th May

Super-excited!

I can't wait for tomorrow.

I picked the **p e r f e c t** outfit.

All shiny and new.

♥

# Monday
## 9th May

I might have drooled slightly today.

But I saw Mark again.

We talked.

It went like this:

He kind of said: 'Hi.'

I kind of said: '*Gulp.*'

Ally thought it was funny.


Why couldn't I say something smart?
Like my name.

Or, 'Hi, you're cute.'

But my heart raced.

My palms were sweaty.

My stomach churned.


Mark must think I've got the IQ of a
goldfish.

O yeah, Ally said I looked like one,
too.

She was talking about my special
outfit.

'Too much gold, Lily. Tone it down.
You look like a freakin' goldfish.'

Who needs friends?

♥

# Tuesday
## 10<sup>th</sup> May

Mark ignored me.

Even though I accidentally bumped into him (on purpose).

Why did I do it?

Is there something like a group meeting for girls who like Mark Ward?

Markoholics Anonymous – or MA?

I need to find out.
Urgently!

I can't keep on doing and saying
stupid things.

♥

# Wednesday
## 11ᵗʰ May

Oops, I did it again.

I walked right up to Mark in the cafeteria.

His new friends were with him.

But I didn't mind. I was full of confidence.

'I like your muscles,' I said.

Or rather, that's what I *wish* I'd said.

Instead I stuttered: 'I like your Brussels … um … sprouts. I like your Brussels sprouts.'

He was eating a hamburger and chips.

Mark frowned.

Even that was sexy.

But I totally blew it with him.

♥

# Thursday
## 12th May

'You're obviously stupid, Lily,' said Ally.

She tried to explain what she meant.
    'You're not always that way. Only
when you're around cute guys.'

Then Ally came up with a plan.

❉   Ignore Mark for a while.

What? Is that *all*?

Is she trying to ruin my love life?

Not that I HAVE a love life. But I won't

if I follow her advice.

   *NEVER*, **EVER**, ***EVER!***

♥

# Friday
## 13th May

I followed Ally's advice. I ignored Mark
the whole day.

It didn't work.
He didn't even glance in my direction.

I probably should've known better – it was Friday the 13th after all.

Here comes the weekend.

Lonely.
Depressed.

**Blingless**.

♥

# Saturday
## 14th May

**08:11**    I decided to make my OWN plan.

**10:45**    No plan came to mind.

**14:08**    Still nothing.

**15:23**     Nope, nothing.

**17:55**     It's hopeless. I'm going to die a spinster.

**20:31**     Are you kidding me? Still nothing.

**22:01**     Going to sleep now.

♥

# Sunday
## 15th May

I made a plan!

My life is **SOOO** about to change.

**WOO-HOO!**


I am going to write Mark a letter.

Yeah, I know it's kind of old-fashioned.

But if I can't TALK to him, I'll WRITE to him.

I'll woo him with my sweet and shiny words.

I ♥ you Mark!
(You just don't know it yet.)

♥

# Monday
## 16th May

**06:30**    I'm dead tired. ZZZ!

But I have to go to school.

I didn't sleep a wink.

I stayed up all night writing

and rewriting Mark's letter.

**06.35**   I read the finished letter
            again.
            *What?*
            Was I on a sugar high?
            I'll try writing again tonight.

**22:17**   Tossed out the previous
            letter. And tried again.

            This one is perfect.
            Not a word is out of place.

            I stuffed the letter in one of
            Mum's best envelopes. And
            decorated the front with
            glitter glue hearts.

I wrote Mark's name as well
– in red glitter glue.

**22:19**   I still feel like the letter needs
something extra …

**AAH! GOT IT!**

**22:21**   I added a humongous
scoop of **VERY PINK, VERY
SHINY** glitter to the
envelope.

If that doesn't get Mark's
attention, nothing will.

**22:23**   A final touch: a shiny sticker

to seal the envelope. And
to seal my love to the best
boy **EVER**.

**22:24**     Going to bed now.
         YAWN!

♥

# Tuesday
## 17<sup>th</sup> May

**OH NO!**

The WORST thing **EVER** happened.

I can barely put it to words.

OK, I'll try.

But first:

**WARNING**: TAKE A DEEP BREATH.

UPSETTING DETAILS TO FOLLOW.

I arrived at school this morning. Mark was already there, talking to his friends.

I smiled at him.

He looked confused.

It probably wasn't my best smile. (Note to self: *Practise your smile, Lily Turner.*)

My love letter to Mark was still in my bag.

He wouldn't be confused for much longer.

My letter said it all:

I 💗 you, Mark Ward.

That, and all the other soppy stuff.


Mark and I didn't talk.

I waited till the time was right. Then I slipped the letter into his bag.

There was no turning back now.

(Unfortunately.)


I kept my eye on Mark the whole day.

We were in English class when he found my letter.

That sexy frown appeared again.

He glanced around.

I pretended to be busy with something else.

But I was **SO** anxious.

*Open it, Mark. Open it, my love!* my mind screamed.

He did.

Or at least he *tried* to.

There were two problems.

* ❋ The incredibly sticky glue of the envelope.
* ❋ The sticker I sealed the envelope with.

He couldn't get the freakin' letter open!

He tried and tried.

Eventually Mark just ripped the whole thing open.

**NOOOO!**

A cloud of pink glitter shot into the air. It was mesmerizing. Almost wonderful ...

... at first.

But then it rained down on Mark.

There was glitter in his hair.

On his face.

On his hands.

In his ears.

On his clothes.

INSIDE his clothes.

**PINK FREAKIN' GLITTER EVERYWHERE!**

Everybody stared. Then they laughed.

I watched in horror.

Mark tried to shake the glitter off. That didn't help. He shined like a pink mirror ball.

I was in **BIG** trouble.

At least he didn't know I was the one who'd slipped him the letter.

*The letter* ...

It fell to the floor when all of this was going on.

I could secretly try and grab it.

And Mark would never know who was responsible.

But he got to the letter before me.

He unfolded it ...

I watched his eyes move across the page. He didn't read my sweet words of love.

Instead his gaze dropped to the signature below.

'LILY TURNER! I'M GOING TO KILL YOU!' he yelled.

Totally **not** the reaction I was expecting.

♥

# Wednesday
## 18th May

There is trouble in paradise.

Mark managed to wash some of the glitter off.

But not all.

The rest seems to have fused into his skin. And into his hair.

Flashes of light shoot from him all the time now. He sparkles and shines whenever he moves.

The worst of all: kids are now calling him **Glitter Boy**.

I kind of like it.
But I really shouldn't.

He gave me an evil glittery glare this morning.

♥

# Thursday
## 19th May

Oops!

Glitter Boy is still shining like the Northern Star.

He had taken something like ten showers since Tuesday.

Of course, I wasn't there to witness it.

That is what people say.

He plans on shaving off all his hair too.

**NOOOOO, GLITTER BOY!**

♥

# Friday
## 20th May

I tried talking to Glitter Boy ... sorry, Mark.

He won't have it. I keep on getting that angry glare.

What?

I'm sure the glitter will all wash off by Monday.

I wonder: Is it too soon to ask if he's read my letter?

I still ♥ him.

♥

# Saturday
## 21st May

I practised my smile this morning.

It worked best when I put on some shiny lip gloss.

Later Ally and I went to the movies.

We saw Glitter Boy there.

He was alone.

♥

# Sunday
## 22nd May

Why was Glitter Boy alone at the movies?

I couldn't work it out.

I thought about it all day.

Then Ally sent me a text.

*His friends abandoned him.*

*Shiny + Pink + Boy = Gay*

♥

# Monday
## 23rd May

It is all such a mess.

I know Mark isn't gay.
Of course, there wouldn't be anything wrong if he were.
But he's not.

And to spread rumours is not cool.

Some kids are so cruel.

(Note to self: *Lily Turner, you made this mess. You'll have to fix it. Even if it means making a further fool of yourself.*)

♥

# Tuesday
## 24th May

I saw Mark again today. He seemed depressed.

Alone, still.

My heart just sank.

'Hold my bag, will you?' I asked Ally.
She didn't know what was going on.
There was no time to explain.

I headed straight to Mark. My heart
was thumping inside my chest.

'Glitter Boy,' I said as loudly as I could.
The school quad suddenly fell silent.
All eyes were on us.

Mark raised his head. I saw the angry
glint in his eyes.
But I pushed through with my plan.

' ... meet Glitter Girl!' I continued,

emptying a packet of pink glitter on my head.

The stuff was everywhere.
There was glitter in my hair.
On my face.
On my hands.
In my ears.
On my clothes.
INSIDE my clothes.

I stood there with my head held high.

❋ Scared of what Mark might do or say.

❋ Scared of the other kids laughing at me.

❋   Scared of being rejected by
        everybody, just like Glitter Boy.

Mark stood up.
He frowned that sexy frown.

Then the anger faded in his eyes.
A slight smile tugged at the corner of
his lips. He shook his head.

'Lily ... You're kind of crazy, you
know?'
'I know,' I said.
'You didn't have to do that.'
'Yes, I did. I wanted to show you that
I care. And that I'm sorry.'

He shuffled around, dropping his gaze.

He seemed at a loss for words.

When our eyes met again, Mark's smile grew bigger.

'You're not going to get all that stuff off,' he said.

His voice was tender.

'Bummer,' I answered and smiled too. The smile I'd practised in front of the mirror on Saturday.

Then he stepped closer.

There were still a few specks of pink glitter in his hair.

'Yup, you are kind of crazy, Glitter Girl,' he said.


He raised his hand.

His fingers touched my face. Gently wiping away some of the glitter.

Then something unexpected happened.

Mark leaned in and kissed me.

Nothing wet. Nothing wild.

Just a gentle kiss.


And when he drew his head back ... there was glitter stuck to his lips.

♥

# Wednesday
## 25th May

It is all new to me.

My first boyfriend **ever**.

OK, perhaps I'm getting ahead of
myself.

Mark and I need to get to know each other.

But I like him.

**A LOT!**

He gives me a shiny, happy feeling inside.

What more could a Glitter Girl wish for?

❋ Perhaps more of those soft kisses.

❋ Perhaps somebody to hold my hand at the movies.

❋ Perhaps somebody who'll one day say: 'I ♥ you Glitter Girl.'

And life would be great.

No, life would be **perfect**.

I  you Glitter Boy!

♥ ♥ ♥ ♥ ♥

# MORE GREAT READS IN THE PROMISES SERIES

### Picture Him

by Jo Cotterill

Aliya loves taking photos. She talks with a stammer, but who needs words when you have pictures?

But when Aliya looks at her latest series of photos ('zombie princess', taken with her friend Zoe) she sees a murky figure in the background of many of them. Is she being stalked?

### ch@t

by Barbara Catchpole

'Are you out of your tiny looney-tunes mind?'

That's what Gina's sister says when she finds out Gina is chatting online with a boy she doesn't know.

But Gina loves talking to Chatboy1 – he makes her laugh and he *understands* her. But what will happen when Gina tries to meet him IRL?